TOPPY
AND THE
CIRCUIT RIDER

TOPPY

AND THE

CIRCUIT RIDER

Barnett Spratt

ILLUSTRATED BY LEONARD VOSBURGH

New York   ABINGDON PRESS   *Nashville*

To all the boys and girls
I have taught
in church and public school

Contents

I	ON THICKETTY MOUNTAIN	9
II	TOPPY'S WISH	21
III	NIGHT IN THE FOREST	34
IV	INDIAN VISITORS	42
V	RIVER BEND	48
VI	TOPPY FINDS OUT	56
VII	CRADDOCK'S CROSSING	63
VIII	NEW FRIENDS	71
IX	MAROONED AGAIN	79
X	SPRINGTIME	85
XI	"GOOD WORK, DAVID"	91
XII	LOST	96
XIII	RATTLESNAKE COVE	103
XIV	SALISBURY TOWN	110
XV	TOPPY'S DECISION	117

The stranger pulled his horse to a stop.

CHAPTER ONE

On Thicketty Mountain

Ten-year-old Toppy Hall hurried up the path from the spring, sloshing water from a battered wooden bucket over his bare feet and buckskin breeches.

"Somebody's comin' on a horse!" he called to the man felling a tree at the edge of the forest. The big backwoodsman walked to the top of the trail, ax in hand. Toppy followed him and waited till the horseman rode into view.

"Howdy," said the stranger as he pulled his horse to a stop. "Can you take me in for the night? I am a traveling preacher, a circuit rider."

"Light and hitch your hoss," answered Pa Brame. "Over thar whar he kin git some grass. Don't have no corn to spare with nine mouths to feed."

The preacher swung from his saddle and shook hands with Pa Brame and Toppy. It was Toppy's first handshake. It left his fingers tingling. He stood still for a moment and stared at the man with the big horse before he hurried to the cabin to break the news to the family.

When he told Granny, she smoothed her ragged apron over her faded dress, gave a twist to her straggly hair, and sat down in her chair by the hearth. The five young Brames crowded the doorway. Ma Brame was at the fireplace stirring a mixture of corn meal, water, and salt that would be their supper. She poured it into hot fat in a skillet and set it on a bed of coals to bake.

"You young'uns git out the door," she said as she turned and wiped her hands on her dress.

The young Brames backed away as Pa Brame came in, followed by the preacher who was head and shoulders taller than his host. The stranger removed his broad-brimmed hat and ducked his head as he crossed the threshold. It was still daylight outside, but inside the cabin it was dark except for the light that came in the open door and from the blaze in the fireplace that extended across one end of the small, crowded room.

Toppy pushed a three-legged stool toward the fire.

The stranger took off his long cape and hung it and his hat on a peg on the wall before he sat down. He had left his saddle, saddlebags, ax, and blanket roll on the end of the log that served for a step into the cabin. Pa Brame laid the man's gun alongside his own on the pegs over the door.

"Howdy," chirped Granny, always ready to talk. "What might be your name?"

"Daniel Wilson. And yours?"

"I was a Wainwright afore I married Cy Hall. I been a Hall ever since. They call me Granny."

"Folks call me Mr. Dan," said the preacher with a friendly smile that showed two rows of strong white teeth.

Toppy stood half hidden in the chimney corner, watching the visitor's face and listening intently as the preacher answered Granny's questions.

"No, this is the first time I have been on Thicketty Mountain. I am a traveling preacher. I came from Charleston, down in the low country. I have been visiting and preaching in these parts for several months. I missed your cabin till today."

Preacher, circuit rider, Charleston? The strange words added to the excitement Toppy had felt since his first glimpse of this tall young man.

The corn pone was soon brown and crisp. Ma Brame broke off a piece for the preacher, then a piece for Pa Brame and Granny. The rest she divided among the five young Brames and Toppy, leaving a small piece for herself. They ate in silence.

When they had all drunk from the bucket Toppy had brought from the spring, the visitor took a flute from his pocket and began to play a tune. Pa Brame eased himself down on the doorstep, and the silent young Brames scrouged in beside him. Ma Brame sat on one of the two three-legged stools. Granny rocked back and forth in her chair by the fire, a pleased smile on her wrinkled face. Toppy left his corner and moved slowly toward the circuit rider, drawn by the music. To Toppy it sounded like the songs of birds he heard in the forest.

There was a hush in the cabin when the preacher stopped playing, put his flute back in his pocket, and took out his Bible. "I will read a portion of God's word," he said, "before we sleep."

Holding the book so the light from the fire fell on the page, he read words that were strange to the ears of his listeners. Like many other families in the

Carolina back country in the year 1790, they had never before heard anyone read from the Bible.

The three little Brames were asleep at the preacher's feet when he finished. There was just room enough for him to kneel and pray. He lifted one child as he rose from his knees, singing softly.

Toppy looked at Granny. There was a faraway look in her eyes as if she were trying to remember something. He had never seen her so quiet. Then Toppy was aware of the preacher looking at them both. The firelight playing over their faces had revealed a striking likeness between them. The tall slender boy and the stooped old woman had the same deep-set blue eyes, high forehead, and firm chin.

Twelve-year-old Joady Brame climbed the ladder to the loft that extended over half the room and threw down a pile of skins. Pa Brame put a bearskin in front of the fire for the preacher to sleep on, and tossed one on the narrow bunk that was Granny's bed. Toppy helped Ma Brame spread the rest on the floor in the space that was left. The preacher laid the little boy in his arms on the nearest one. The two youngsters on the floor were roused and crawled whimpering over beside him. Toppy and Buddy, the second Brame boy, climbed the ladder and joined Joady in the loft.

Joady and Buddy were soon asleep. The circuit rider, too, was asleep with his saddlebags for a pillow. But Toppy lay awake thinking about this man from the outside world. What quar clothes he wears! What is a preacher? Why did he come? How long 'll he stay?

At dawn next morning Toppy peeped over the edge of the loft. The stranger, with his saddlebags under his arms, was tiptoeing out of the cabin, taking care not to step on any of the sleeping Brames.

"I'll see whar he's gwine," Toppy said to himself as he slid quietly down the ladder against the wall.

He saw the stranger untie his horse and start down the path to the spring. Gwine to water his horse, Toppy decided as he followed them at a safe distance.

He drew closer when he saw the preacher take off his shirt, wash it, and hang it on a bush to dry. While his horse was drinking from the spring branch, he washed his face, hands, and hair, and splashed water over his bare shoulders. When the man took a clean shirt out of his saddlebags and pulled it over his head, Toppy's curiosity took him still nearer. The few men and boys he knew had only one buckskin or homespun shirt at a time and wore it day and night summer and winter till it wore out. He continued to stare as the preacher put on his long waistcoat and tight-fitting coat that buttoned up to his neck.

"Why, good morning," called Mr. Dan when he turned and saw Toppy. "I didn't know anybody was up but me. My, this water is cold! But how good it makes a man feel!"

Toppy's hand went to the locust thorn that held his ragged shirt together. To his surprise he felt a sudden desire to splash the cold water on his unwashed body. I'll do it another day, he decided.

When Daniel Wilson combed the tangles from his thick reddish-brown hair that hung loose to his shoulders, Toppy winced. He remembered the last time Granny struggled with his unruly, sun-bleached hair before she got it braided tight and tied it with a rawhide thong.

"Would you like to ride Big Gray up the hill?" the preacher asked. Without waiting for an answer, he put his hands under Toppy's elbows and tossed him up on the horse's back. Toppy was surprised to find how at home he felt astride the big animal. He wished the path to the cabin were longer.

"Like to ride?" the preacher asked when he helped him down. Toppy's shining eyes and slow, shy smile answered better than words.

The bearskins were back in the loft, and Ma Brame had corn bread and fried pork on the hearth for breakfast. "Come eat," she called. Again the meal was finished in silence.

"Two axes are better than one," the circuit rider said as he joined Pa Brame at the tree he was felling.

The tall pine soon came down with a crash. It took the best part of the morning to cut it into firewood. Toppy and Joady helped stack the logs near the rock chimney and piled the chips under the cabin. There was more corn bread and fried meat and fresh water from the spring when they had finished.

The circuit rider stood in front of the fireplace and preached a brief sermon, sang a hymn, and prayed. Toppy liked the sound of his voice, especially his singing.

"But what do hit all mean? Do Granny know?" he said to himself.

He watched her face as the preacher read again from the little book in his pocket. She still had that faraway, questioning look in her eyes.

16

As the preacher closed his Bible, Granny clapped her bony hands and exclaimed, "I remember now! I remember jist like hit was yestiddy! Toppy, stan' on my bed and feel for Pa's book!" She pointed to the overhead beam in the corner. "I had done plum' forgot hit was up thar."

Toppy ran his hand along the log beam and brought down a ragged, dusty bundle. Out of it Granny took a small calf-bound book with two brass clasps.

"This here was my pa's," she said. "He could git the words out'n it! I was jist five years old. He set in the chair by the fire, and I set in his lap! He could git the words out jist like you're doin', Mr. Dan!"

She put the little Bible in his hand. On the flyleaf he read, *David Wainwright, Bristol, England, 1730.*

"And here is a letter," he added, carefully unfolding a sheet of paper that was yellow and brittle with age. "The ink is so faded I can make out only a part of it."

Toppy's eyes widened with interest as the circuit rider read slowly:

> May he who guided you from your youth up continue to preserve your health and strengthen your faith as you leave these shores for the New World. This is the prayer, dear David, of
>
> Your affectionate servant and teacher,
> Christopher Clement
>
> To David Wainwright, Bristol, England
>
> December 7, 1730

"Yes, David Wainwright wuz my pa's name, an' my boy Dave's, an' hit's Toppy's." Granny placed her hand on Toppy's arm. "We call him Toppy.

"Them's all Brames," she explained waving a hand toward the five stocky, black-haired children and their parents. "They hain't no kin to Toppy and me. But this here cabin wuz mine. I give hit to Cal Brame, thar, to take kere o' me. I borned seven babies here. None of 'em lived to be growed cept'n Hank and Dave. Hits been more'n three years since I seen Hank. Don' know whar he is now.

"When Toppy's mammy died, his pappy, my boy Dave, brought 'im here to me. Lef' 'im and went on down yon mountins."

After a pause she added, "He never come back. Got killed in a war battle called King's Mountin, Charley Crouch said. Hain't nobody lef' here but Toppy an' me." She took the little calf-bound book and the letter and wrapped them in the faded cloth they had lain in for half a century.

Toppy had heard Granny talk of his father and hers, but this was the first time she had mentioned the little bundle. And even his sharp eyes had never seen it hidden high up on the beam in the corner. But that was not what he wondered about. What he wanted to know was how the stranger got words out of

Granny's pa's book and out of the one in his pocket and off that old piece of paper.

It was mid-afternoon when the traveling preacher said he must be on his way. "I will come again some day," he promised as he rode down the trail.

"An' he will. I know he will," Toppy said to himself.

CHAPTER TWO

Toppy's Wish

Soon after the preacher's visit heavy frosts and high winds stripped chestnuts, maples, hickories, and beeches of their crimson and gold leaves. Winter was near. There was work to be done on Thicketty Mountain.

"You young'uns, all o' you, go fetch mud from the creek bank to daub up them cracks round that door and back o' Granny's bed," Pa Brame said one morning.

Toppy, Joady, Buddy, and even seven-year-old Ronny helped fill a crude leather bucket with red mud from the edge of the stream. It took Pa Brame's strong arm to carry the bucket up the hill. The boys talked about their recent visitor as they patted the mud into the chinks. Buddy wished he had a horse like the circuit rider's.

"Me, too," said Joady, "then me an' Pa could ride to the tradin' pos' and take —"

"I'd go too," interrupted Buddy. "I wished first."

"An' me too," chimed in Ronny.

"I'd shore like a gun like his'n," Joady went on wishing. "I could kill a buck or a bar with a rifle."

Toppy wished for a rifle, too. He did not add that what he wished most was to find out how the preacher got words out of Granny's pa's book.

The next day's job was gathering chestnuts from the burs that the frost had burst wide open. They would be stored in a corner of the loft for food in the winter. Buddy and Ronny soon turned back with their load, but Toppy and Joady went on from tree to tree till they were some distance from the cabin. The leather bags hung across their shoulders were full of nuts when Toppy stopped suddenly.

"Look, look, Joady!" he whispered, pointing to a huge cinnamon bear measuring his great height with his claws on the trunk of a tree. The sight sent the two boys scrambling down the mountain side, scattering nuts as they ran.

"Pa, Pa!" they shouted. "Pa, a bar, a bar! A big 'un! We seen 'im standin' 'ginst a tree."

"You young'uns an' your ma stay here till I kill 'im," Pa Brame said as he loaded his gun and hung his ax and hunting knife in his belt. "Then you kin come an' help."

Ma Brame and the four boys waited at the edge of the clearing until Pa Brame called. He was hacking off the head of the great beast when they reached the spot.

"Fat an' lazy," he said. "One shot got 'im."

"I reckon mebby he was on his way to his den for the winter," commented Toppy.

Pa Brame cut a strong pole and braced it in the crotch of two trees. Small saplings thrust under the heavy body helped them to lift it to the pole. The hind legs were tied to it with stout grapevines. Pa Brame carefully slit the shaggy pelt with his hunting knife so that it could be taken off in one piece. A good bed hit'll make when hit's scraped and dried 'ginst the cabin wall, Toppy was thinking. For Granny, I hope.

When the big carcass was dismembered and quartered, they had to make several trips to carry it all to the cabin. Bear steaks that night for supper! Then the rest was smoked in the wide chimney and hung from the rafters over the loft to be eaten as needed.

23

It was snowing two weeks later when Pa Brame got back from the trading post ten miles away where he had taken the pelts of the small animals — otter, muskrat, red fox, and mink — caught in his traps during the fall. He had traded them for salt, powder and shot, and a length of homespun cloth.

This first snow was followed by others. It was a hard winter on Thicketty Mountain. When it rained, the ground froze, and great trees crashed under the weight of the ice on their branches. Cold blasts rushed into the cabin when the door was opened to bring in wood for the fire. There were few sunny days, and Toppy was glad when one did come. Then he and Joady and Buddy went with Pa Brame to look at the trap lines along the banks of Thicketty Creek, or trudged through the snow with him hunting rabbits and squirrels. Pa Brame would load his old flintlock and let each one of them shoot it. Toppy could bring down his squirrel every time.

The family was sometimes snowed indoors for days at a time. They got in each other's way, fussing and quarreling and fighting as they crowded near the fire to keep warm.

"I done tole you young'uns to git back," Ma Brame

would scold when she was cooking at the fire.

Up the ladder Toppy, Joady, and Buddy would scuttle, but not before the last one got a whack with the stick Ma Brame used to poke the fire. This was seldom Toppy, for he was faster than the Brame boys.

They were all afraid of Pa Brame's temper and of the rawhide strap he kept handy and used freely.

"Hit hain't my time to bring in wood," Joady said one morning. "Hit's your'n, Toppy."

"I done brung in two loads since you did," Toppy answered.

"Then hit's Buddy's," said Joady.

"Hit hain't neither. I brung in the water, didn't I, Ma?"

This argument as usual ended with Pa Brame giving them all a thrashing with the rawhide strap.

Granny had a bad cough and a pain in her chest all that winter which kept her in bed most of the time. Toppy heated smooth rocks in the fire and put them at her feet to keep her warm. One day when she felt better, he sat on the bed beside her. They talked about the preacher and puzzled over the little black marks on the yellowed pages of her pa's Bible. Toppy liked the feel of the soft calf-skin cover.

"Yes, my pa could git the words out'n it, same as the preacher," Granny began. She recalled again the dim picture she had in her mind of her father.

The Brames were not interested, but Toppy loved the tale. "How did the words git in the books," he asked himself. "An' how did Granny's pa and Mr. Dan git 'em out?"

He snapped the two brass clasps shut and held the litttle volume tight against his chest. "Some day I aim to fin' out," he said aloud.

"What, Toppy? What you aim to fin' out?" asked Granny.

"How to git words out this here book," he answered.

Joady and Buddy laughed but Granny said, "I reckon mebby you will, an' I reckon mebby you'll be goin' down yon mountins when you're a growed-up man to see what's on tother side. Pa brung me and my ma from some'eres over thar when I wuz a teency lettle young'un. Ole Miss Ludie—who took me when Pa died, you know — tole me my ma died when I wuz no more'n a year ole.

"No, she never tole me nothin' mo' 'bout Pa and Ma, 'cep'n they come from a furaway place call Philly-delfy. She was a shut-mouth woman, Ole Miss Ludie

26

Toppy and Granny puzzled over the little black marks.

wuz, an' she didn't 'low me to ast no questions. She mouta' had somethin' b'long'd to my ma, but all she give me when I married Cy Hall wuz this here book o' Pa's.

"Hit's your'n when I'm gone," she added when Toppy had put it back in its place.

Spring came early to the Carolina mountains that year. Flowers bloomed at the woods' edge and along the creek bank. The birds Toppy had missed all winter came back to build their nests. He had his own names for all of them and could imitate their calls.

"Joady, come!" he called one day, "I done foun' 'nother bobwhite nest."

As they neared the nest, the mother bird flew up in their faces. Pretending a broken wing, she flopped about trying to lead them astray. The boys laughed.

"She's tryin' to fool us," said Toppy.

Down on their knees they looked into the nest she had hollowed out in a mound of pine needles.

"Two or three birds must a' layed to her," said Joady when he saw the pile of eggs in the nest. "Put 'em in my cap. Ma'll bile 'em fur dinner like she done them duck eggs we foun' on the creek bank."

Toppy carefully placed the snow-white eggs in the coonskin cap. "The mos' we ever foun' in one nes'," he said. "Granny 'll be proud."

Bird-nesting, chopping wood, and fishing with Joady and Buddy filled Toppy's days. But he often thought of the circuit rider's promise to come back to Thicketty Mountain.

"Why don' he come?" he said to himself again and again. Then he would think of all the dangers of traveling alone in the wilderness — snow and ice in winter, swollen streams, wild animals, savage Indians, ruffians, and robbers.

It was October again. Toppy had almost given up hope of the circuit rider's return when one afternoon he heard a horse whinnying at the foot of the trail.

"He's a-comin'! He's a-comin'!" he shouted to Joady and Buddy. "Hit's 'im! Hit's the preacher and his big horse! I knowed he'd come!"

Everybody was at the top of the trail or in the doorway to meet the circuit rider. Everybody but Granny. Her cough was worse, and she was too weak to get out of bed. Toppy ran ahead to tell her the good news.

"Granny, the preacher's done come back! Mr. Dan's here, Granny!" he was whispering to her softly when

29

the circuit rider and the Brames entered the cabin.

Granny opened her eyes and smiled. "Howdy, Mr. Dan," she said feebly.

The circuit rider took her scrawny wrist in his strong hand and felt her racing pulse.

"Get a bucket of water, Toppy," he said as he opened his saddlebags and took out a towel, a pewter cup, and a packet of powders.

When Toppy came back from the spring, the preacher raised Granny's head and gave her one of the powders in a cup of water. "This will make you feel better, Granny," he said.

All through the night he sat by her bed and bathed her face with the cool spring water. Toppy sat on the floor at the foot of her bed. Ma Brame did not lie down. Twice she went with Toppy to the spring to get water. The rest of the family slept on their bearskins.

In her delirium Granny muttered, "My pa could git words out the book." Again and again she repeated it and added, "Toppy 'll git the words out o' hit too someday."

She grew weaker and weaker. At daybreak Toppy was asleep. Ma Brame shook him gently. "Granny's dead," she said simply.

The preacher laid a friendly hand on his shoulder. Ma Brame waked the rest of the family and went about cooking corn bread for breakfast.

They buried Granny on the hillside that afternoon as the sun was sinking behind the mountains. The preacher read the burial service, sang a hymn, and prayed. Toppy lingered awhile after the others had walked back to the cabin. Thicketty Mountain without Granny! A lump rose in his throat. What would become of him, he wondered.

In the middle of the night he choked back his sobs lest he wake Joady and Buddy. "I don' b'long to nobody now," he said to himself.

Next morning he heard the preacher talking to Pa and Ma Brame.

"And the boy has no other kin?" he was asking.

"His pa's brother, Hank," answered Pa Brame. "He mus' be livin' over thar som'ers but I don' know whar. Granny 'lowed once that Hank would take 'im when she wuz gone."

"As I travel through these mountains," said the circuit rider, "I can inquire. Perhaps I can locate Hank Hall."

"Lessen you kin I'll have to keep Toppy, I reckon,

31

till he's growed. But he ain't got no claim on me, and I got five young 'uns o' my own to raise," complained Pa Brame.

"I might take Toppy with me," suggested the circuit rider. "If we do not find his uncle, I can bring him here or perhaps find another home for him."

"Hit would be one less mouth to feed," mumbled Pa Brame.

"Leave hit to him," Ma Brame said. "If'n he wants to go he kin."

"Yes," said the circuit rider, "I think the decision should be left to him."

Toppy stood still and tense. It would be wonderful to ride with Mr. Dan on Big Gray's back. And maybe Mr. Dan would read to him. But how could he leave Joady and Buddy and all he had known since he could remember? What would become of him if he went, or if he stayed? What would Granny want him to do? He turned suddenly, walked up the hillside, and stood for a little while by Granny's grave.

When he came back, he had decided. "Mr. Dan," he said breathing hard, "I'm a-goin' with you."

And so it was settled. The preacher saddled Big

Gray, adjusted the saddlebags and blanket roll, hung his short-handled ax and powder horn on the pommel of the saddle, and put his rifle over his shoulder. Then he shook hands with Ma and Pa Brame, put his hand on the head of each of the children, and gave them all his blessing. Toppy stood ready with the little calf-bound Bible in his hand, the only thing from the cabin that he owned.

"I will keep it safe for you," said Mr. Dan. He took the Bible from its faded wrappings and put it in one of the spacious pockets of his waistcoat where he kept his own. When he was in the saddle, Pa Brame lifted Toppy up behind. There were no good-bys as they rode away, but Toppy kept looking back as long as he could see the last wisp of smoke from the cabin chimney.

CHAPTER THREE

Night in the Forest

Big Gray carried them along a hatchet-blazed trail that wound around the foot of Thicketty Mountain. Toppy remembered his brief ride from the spring to the cabin on Big Gray's back.

"Now, I'll be a-ridin' and a-ridin'!" he said to himself. "Might be I'll git a chance to fin' out how he gits words out them two books."

He touched Big Gray with both hands to make sure the horse was real — that it was not all just a dream.

"I wish Granny knowed," he said to himself.

The thought of Granny brought a wave of homesickness.

"Mr. Dan said he'd take me back if'n we don' fin' Granny's boy Hank. But will Hank want me if'n we do fin' 'im? I wish I b'longed to somebody."

It was late afternoon when the preacher called over

his shoulder, "There must be a spring at the head of this stream. We will follow it and see."

In a few minutes they came upon it, bubbling out of the side of the mountain. "As good a place as we may find to spend the night," he said. "We must have a fire going before dark."

When they had had a drink of water, Mr. Dan began to chop wood for a fire. Toppy gathered dry brushwood. The fire in the cabin on Thicketty Mountain had never been allowed to go out summer or winter as long as Toppy could remember, and he had never built an outdoor fire. He watched as the fire was made and listened carefully to the circuit rider's explanation.

"First, a heavy, solid backlog; two sticks at right angles to it; between them a pile of dry twigs and strips of birch bark. A spark from my steel and flint starts the blaze and keeps it burning till I add half a dozen hickory logs.

"Fire is man's friend," the circuit rider went on as he added the logs. "The wild animals of the forest are afraid of it and will not come near us as long as there is a blaze. Man alone is not afraid of fire. He has hands to put it out as well as start it. We must always put out our fires when we move on or the woods might burn up.

"Now our bed," he said as he cut thick boughs of pine. "Carry them to that open spot by the fire. Not too close."

Toppy sniffed the fragrant fresh-cut hemlock as he stacked it in a neat pile and added dry leaves. Pine-bough beds were not new to him. When the weather was warm, they had sometimes taken the place of the bearskins in the cabin on Thicketty Mountain.

The circuit rider walked a few yards away with his gun and came back with a squirrel. When it was skinned, dressed, and skewered on a green locust stick, Toppy held it over hot coals to roast. The smell was good. It whetted his appetite.

Will he 'low me to shoot that rifle some? he wondered, remembering his and Joady's wish for one like it.

"Keep turning that squirrel," warned Mr. Dan, "so the juice will stay in."

They ate it with some of the corn bread Ma Brame had wrapped in cornshucks and put in the saddlebags.

"I learned to build fires when I was a soldier in the army, and to make pine-bough beds when I was a

The circuit rider came back with a squirrel.

surveyor in the mountains before I became a circuit rider," Mr. Dan said.

He explained the work of a surveyor and told of encounters with Indians and wild animals. Toppy held his breath as the circuit rider described a fight with a hungry bobcat.

"I never traveled alone then, and I am glad to have a companion again," he added.

"Companion?" Toppy did not know the meaning of the word, but he understood the friendly smile that went with it.

"Toppy, what do you know about your uncle Hank?" asked Mr. Dan.

"Nothin', I just seen him twice when he come to Thicketty Mountin." The look on Toppy's face showed plainly that the picture of Hank Hall which he carried in his mind was not a pleasant one.

"And what did Granny tell you about her pa, your great-grandfather?" continued the circuit rider.

"Nothin', cep'n she set on his lap an' hear-d 'im git words out'n his book. An' she said Ole Miss Ludie, who took her when her pa died, tole her he brung Granny and her ma from a fur off place. Phillidelfy, or some sich name."

"Philadelphia is a city," said Mr. Dan, "a long way from Thicketty Mountain. Many pioneers from England come first to Philadelphia. I have never been there. But I lived in another city — Baltimore — five years ago with my doctor brother, and attended Cokesbury College."

Doctor? Cokesbury? College? Toppy's mountain shyness would not let him ask the questions that were in his mind.

Night came quickly on the densely wooded mountain side. Fresh logs were added to the fire, and a supply of logs was laid nearby. Big Gray was tethered to a sapling.

"Let us pray before we sleep," said the circuit rider.

When at last they were side by side on the hemlock boughs, Toppy lay staring at the heaven full of stars over his head. Owls in the treetops hooted and blinked at the firelight. Wolves howled, and a red fox yapped and snarled over his prey. These were familiar sounds to the mountain boy. He was not afraid, but he missed Granny and the walls of the cabin. He felt a wave of homesickness again and wished he were back in the loft sleeping by Joady and Buddy.

But Pa Brame don' wan' me. Will Granny's boy

Hank wan' me if'n we fin' 'im? he wondered again. The thought of finding his uncle brought no comfort.

Mr. Dan reached over and tucked the blanket snugly around Toppy's shoulder. Soon both were asleep.

The sun was up next morning when the preacher called, "Wake up, Toppy, we must be on our way."

Toppy sat up and rubbed his eyes. "Where am I?" he wondered. It was several moments before he remembered. Mr. Dan was on his knees by the stream washing his hands and face — not his hair and shirt this time.

"Come wash up," he called.

When Toppy joined him, the circuit rider handed him the towel and pointed to the water. Toppy dipped his hands in the stream and rubbed them together. He hesitated a minute before he dipped them in again and rubbed them over his face. Washing-up was not a regular habit with him.

What's he doin' now? Toppy wondered as he watched the circuit rider cut a twig from a black gum tree, fringe one end, wet it, and brush his teeth. He cut a second brush, handed it to Toppy, and explained its use.

"It will make your mouth feel good," he said.

Toppy dipped his brush in the stream and awkwardly applied it to his straight, even teeth. "Hit do feel good," he admitted to himself.

When they had eaten the rest of Ma Brame's corn bread, the preacher read a Psalm from his Bible.

"Toppy, a man named David wrote these words. He was a great king. Some day I will read you his story in Granny's Bible. Your Granny said your name is David. I think I will call you David. It is a good name."

Toppy was confused. How did Granny's pa's name git in Mr. Dan's book? he wondered. And how do Mr. Dan know what's in Granny's pa's book? When'll I fin' out?

The circuit rider studied a scrap of paper. "To the west over the mountain!" he read. "Cross the river in the valley below — follow the valley ten or twelve miles to where the river makes a sharp bend to the left.

"Another preacher traveled this way last year. He gave me these directions to the River Bend settlement. Let's go, Toppy — I mean David."

CHAPTER FOUR

Indian Visitors

Sure-footed Big Gray pushed his way through tangled vines that covered the trail up the mountain side. Toppy took a long, deep breath when they stopped on the summit for a brief rest before they began the rough descent. Range after range of purple-shadowed mountains stretched out before him. He had never before seen so much of the world.

The trail down the mountain on the other side was equally steep and rugged. Twice Mr. Dan had to dismount and cut a way through the dense underbrush. Often Big Gray had to go around great boulders.

When they had reached the river in the valley below, Mr. Dan shook his head. "We can't cross here. Big Gray is a powerful swimmer but in floodtime these rock-bedded streams are dangerous. There has been a heavy rain up the valley."

They rode on several miles but found no place where it was safe to ford the swift stream.

"Looks as if we will have to camp on this side till tomorrow." He tied Big Gray to a limb of a tree and studied the situation. "We will make our bed under that hemlock. It will shelter us if it rains."

A fire was built and enough wood cut for the night.

"We have a long time before dark, David. I will read from Granny's Bible the stories of the two men whose names you and I bear — David and Daniel."

Toppy listened spellbound to the story of the young man named David who with a slingshot and a smooth stone from the brook killed the great giant Goliath. Then he heard the story of Daniel who was thrown into a den of lions. He watched with wonder and curiosity at the way the circuit rider's eyes moved and his hand turned the pages.

"How is he gittin' that talk out'n that book?" Toppy asked himself. "When 'll I fin' out?"

As if he had heard Toppy's question Mr. Dan said, "You must learn to read Granny's Bible for yourself, David. First I will teach you the Lord's Prayer so you can say it with me when we pray together night and morning. Here it is, right here on this page. It will be your reading lesson some day soon."

Mr. Dan repeated the prayer phrase by phrase till Toppy could say it alone. He didn't understand what the words meant, but he enjoyed saying them. He was sorry when the circuit rider closed the book and put it in his pocket.

They gathered chestnuts and black walnuts from the nearby trees and wild grapes from an overhanging vine for their supper. The preacher roasted the chestnuts while Toppy cracked the nuts. Darkness settled down in the valley as the two sat munching hot chestnuts.

"You are not sorry you came with me, are you, David?"

Toppy smiled his slow, shy smile. But before he could answer, two Indians came out of the blackness. Their painted bodies shone in the firelight. The circuit rider quickly took his flute from his pocket and began to play. The unwelcome guests laughed, talked to each other, and touched the flute with their fingers. Suddenly one of them snatched it and disappeared into the forest followed by his companion.

"We must cross the river!" Daniel Wilson whispered. "They may come back any minute and

take my horse and gun! They may even do us harm!"

The circuit rider was saddling Big Gray as he talked. He put Toppy in the saddle and hurriedly pushed the boy's moccasined feet through the loops of the stirrup straps. Then he climbed up behind, his long arms reaching for the reins.

"Hold on tight!" he shouted as he urged Big Gray into the rampaging stream.

The plunge dashed spray over their heads. Big Gray yielded a little with the current and stumbled on the slippery rocks, but finally he swam puffing and snorting to the opposite shore, only to fall back when he tried to clamber up its steep bank. Swinging still farther downstream, he made a second and a third attempt. The third time his front feet clung to the muddy bank long enough for the circuit rider to swing himself up to an overhanging limb. He reached for Toppy. Too late!

Horse and rider went down again into the churning water. Toppy shut his eyes, clamped his knees tighter against the saddle, and hung on with both hands. Up they came again, and this time they made it to solid ground. Terrified and half drowned, Toppy slid off the horse. Mr. Dan dropped from the tree and patted the wet, trembling boy with one hand and the wet, trembling horse with the other.

"We must have a fire to dry ourselves, David. The Indians will not cross that river tonight in a canoe. They are probably trying to get a tune out of my flute and are fighting over possession of it. Lucky it was for us that I had something they wanted at the moment more than my horse and our scalps. But how I do regret the loss of my flute! Hold Big Gray while I hunt some wood."

The sky had cleared and a half moon shed some light in the valley. After what seemed a long time to Toppy, the circuit rider came back with an armful of brushwood. Soon they were drying their clothes by a fire. It was built behind a boulder to shield them from any Indian arrows that might come from the other side of the river.

Toppy tried hard to stay awake, but he did not know when Mr. Dan laid him on a pallet of pine needles. When he waked up next morning, he found that Mr. Dan had not slept. He had spent the night keeping up the brushwood fire and drying the contents of the saddlebags.

"Our powder is dry," he said as he pulled the plug from the mouth of the powder horn. "But my gun and ax are gone. Our Bibles and the other things in my waistcoat pockets did not get wet."

"Mr. Dan," Toppy said softly when they were on Big Gray again, "Mr. Dan."

"Yes, David?"

"I ain't sorry I come. I'm glad."

"I am glad too, David."

CHAPTER FIVE

River Bend

As they rode along, Toppy wondered what they would do without a gun and an ax.

"We got to have a gun to kill rabbits and squir'ls an' a ax to chop wood to cook 'em," he said to himself. "Brushwood fires burns out too quick. An' I did'n git to shoot that rifle."

He was still worrying over the loss when they reached River Bend. Two tow-headed boys leading a cow by a rawhide rope stopped and stared at them. Women and children peered from doorways. Buckskin clad men gathered about Big Gray.

"One of them travelin' preachers, ain't you? Know by them clothes," said one of them.

"Yes," answered Daniel Wilson, as he swung from his saddle. "Where is the best place to have preaching here?"

"Ask Wade Killian thar. He's got the bigges' cabin."

A tall bronzed man with a twinkle in his clear blue eyes came forward and shook hands.

"The folks all come to prayer meetin' at our house," he said. "My wife'll want you to put up with us while you're in River Bend."

"And my companion here, David Hall?" asked the circuit rider, giving Toppy a hand to dismount.

"Both o' you," answered Mr. Killian.

He led the way to a well-built cabin, the only two-room cabin in the settlement. Paper smeared with bear grease covered two small windows and let in a little light.

A pleasant-faced woman rose from the hearth as they entered. "Just in time for dinner," she said, "and proud we are to have you."

Hot johnnycakes and honey, sweet potatoes, squirrel stew with milk gravy. Mrs. Killian gave Toppy bountiful helpings. He had never tasted anything so good.

"Another preacher was here a year ago, Brother Wilson," said Mrs. Killian when dinner was over. "He spent two nights with us and preached four times in this room. We've met regular for prayer meetin' ever since."

Toppy sat quietly and listened as they told Mr. Dan about the weekly prayer meetings.

"They talk jist like Mr. Dan," he said to himself. "Is hit 'cause they kin git words out'n the book?"

He looked about the room with its clean floor, neat hearth, and sturdy split-log table, stools, and fire bench. How different from the crowded cabin back home, he thought.

Word had gotten around that there would be preaching at the Killians, and it was not long before the neighbors began to gather. The two rooms were soon crowded, and the preacher started the service.

"And you lost your gun and ax," said Mr. Killian next morning.

The circuit rider had told them of the narrow escape from the two Indians.

"Mebby old Uncle Sol would sell his," suggested Mrs. Killian. "He's sick and stone blind."

"I would be glad to pay well for them," said Daniel Wilson.

"Don't b'lieve old Sol would part with his gun," said Mr. Killian. "Used to be the best shot in these hills. Keeps that rifle on the bed beside him. But we'll go see him."

"Yes," said Mrs. Killian, "he'll want the preacher to visit him. A good old man. He came to meetin' regular before he got sick."

Toppy went with Mr. Killian and Mr. Dan to see Uncle Sol.

"Brought the preacher to see you," Mr. Killian called from the doorstep.

Uncle Sol sat straight up in bed, his massive head

thrown back and his wide open, sightless, blue eyes staring straight ahead. His snow-white beard covered his chest.

"Come in, come in and set thar on the fire bench. Wade Killian, stir up that fire afore you set."

"This is my young friend, David Hall, Uncle Sol," said Mr. Dan when he had shaken hands.

The old man reached out a gnarled hand and held Toppy's in a tight grip.

"I knowed a boy once name o' Hall. Cy Hall."

"My gran'paw was name Cy Hall," said Toppy.

"Well, well! Cy Hall's gran'son! I never knowed what come o' him."

"Then you would not know of his son Hank's whereabouts," said Daniel Wilson.

"No, Cy wuz jist a boy when I knowed him," answered Uncle Sol.

"How old are you, son?" he asked Toppy.

"Ten," Toppy replied.

"Ten? Jist the age o' my Jim when he died. Bit by a rattler. Hear-d the singin' las' night," he added after a pause. "Line out a hymn tune, preacher, an' I'll sing hit with you."

When they were ready to leave, Mr. Killian told

Uncle Sol about the preacher's losing his gun and ax in his flight from the Indians.

"He would like to buy yours," he added, "if — "

"They hain't fur sale!" interrupted Uncle Sol emphatically. "They hain't fur sale!"

"I would pay you what they are worth," said Daniel Wilson. Uncle Sol reached for his rifle and laid it across his knees.

"They hain't fur sale," he repeated, "but I'm a-givin' you my gun, preacher."

He lifted the rifle and held it out at arms' length till the circuit rider took it from him.

"An' the boy kin have the ax — thar on the hearthstone. Been wantin' to leave 'em both in good hands. Young Sol got his'n. Don' need 'em."

The circuit rider did not offer again to pay for them. Toppy was glad. He felt that Uncle Sol would not have liked it.

The circuit rider had just finished his sermon that afternoon and the congregation was singing the last hymn when a boy near the door shouted, "Fire! Fire! The Widow Pickett's house is afire!"

Mr. Killian took command. "Quiet! Stop! Don't

narry a person move till I tell you! Now walk out that door, then hurry and get your fire buckets!"

Everybody obeyed. Outside they rushed to their cabins for buckets. Toppy stood bewildered till a woman thrust a bucket into his hand and said, "Here, boy, git to work!"

Before he knew what was going on, Toppy was in the fire brigade that reached from the river to the cabin with the roof ablaze. Two men stood waist deep in the river filling bucket after bucket with water. The full buckets were passed from hand to hand up one line to the fire, and the empty ones went down a second line back to the river to be refilled. Men, women, and children sang as the buckets were swung from hand to hand:

"Pass 'em on, pass 'em on!
Faster, faster!
Keep 'em goin'! Keep 'em goin'!
Faster, faster!
Put it out, put it out!"

Toppy joined in the chant and began to enjoy the excitement. Mr. Killian and the circuit rider at the end of the lines kept a constant stream of water pouring on the cabin till the fire was out.

When the commotion was over, the folks went back to their cabins for supper. Only the chimney and side walls of Widow Pickett's home were left standing.

"I reckon mebby Mr. Dan 'll be helpin' fix that roof tomorrow," Toppy said to himself.

That night he heard Mr. Killian tell the circuit rider that Widow Pickett and her five children would sleep around at the neighbors.

"We'll put a new roof on her cabin," he said. "And we might as well build her a loft while we are at it."

"David and I'll stay and help," said the circuit rider.

"I knowed hit," Toppy said to himself. "I knowed he'd stay."

He was not sorry that it took three days to fell the trees and finish the job. It meant three more days of Mrs. Killian's good cooking — hot corn bread, and fried mountain trout that he and the Widow Pickett's boys caught in the river. And there were three more nights of sleeping on a mattress stuffed with corn shucks on a bunk built against the cabin wall — another first experience for Toppy. He wondered the last night if he would ever be so comfortable again.

CHAPTER SIX

Toppy Finds Out

"I hope we can make it to Craddock's Crossing by night. There's a tavern there where we can get a place to sleep," the circuit rider said. It was noon of the day they finally left River Bend. They had stopped to eat some of the lunch Mrs. Killian had given them.

"How fur?" asked Toppy.

"One man said twenty, another fifteen miles. We can make good time as long as we follow this trace, but the going will be slower when we turn off on the trail over Buckeye Mountain that leads to Craddock's Crossing."

Soon after they started up the mountain trail, dense clouds darkened the heavens. Sharp flashes of lightning and loud claps of thunder followed each other in frightening succession. First big drops and then a deluge of rain came down in great sheets.

Mr. Dan hastily dismounted and led Big Gray under an oak tree.

"It will soon be over," he shouted to Toppy above the noise. "A mountain storm."

The terrific wind bent tall pine trees till they swept the ground. It uprooted a giant oak and sent it crashing down the mountain side. Toppy sat on Big Gray and watched the mighty spectacle without fear.

In an hour the violence of the storm was over as suddenly as it began, and the rain settled into a steady downpour.

"We must try to find a better shelter," said the circuit rider as he swung back in the saddle. "We may come to a cabin further on."

They had ridden a mile or two when Toppy called, "Thar's one! Thar's a cabin!"

"Where?" asked Mr. Dan pulling Big Gray to a stop.

"Over thar, 'hind them bushes and trees," said Toppy. "No smoke," he added.

"Which means nobody at home," finished Mr. Dan.

They both dismounted and made their way to the cabin.

"A hunter's shack, likely," said the circuit rider as

he pushed back the sagging bearskin that served as a door. "Looks as if he has not been at home for a good while."

With a branch from a nearby tree, he began to sweep out the dead leaves that half filled the small room.

"Tie Big Gray near the door, David, while I clear out this trash so we can get inside."

When their eyes had become accustomed to the darkness, they saw wood stacked against the wall.

"If this rain continues, we will have to spend the night," said Mr. Dan. "May as well have a fire."

Soon the dry hickory and chestnut wood left by the hunter was crackling in the fireplace, giving out light and warmth. Mr. Dan sat down on a log and made room for Toppy beside him. When they had eaten the rest of their lunch, except two corn pones left for breakfast, he took Granny's Bible from his pocket.

"You know these words by heart, David," he said, turning to the Lord's Prayer. "Now you can learn them by sight."

Toppy's eyes were bright and his voice eager as he called the words Mr. Dan touched with a twig, first as they came and then skipping about.

"Good!" said the circuit rider. "Now I'll teach you your letters. There are twenty-six you must know. Twenty-two of them are in this prayer. Here is the first one, *a*. See how many times you can find *a*. Now, *b*. Now, *c*. And *d*."

In a short while Toppy could say the letters of the alphabet and recognize most of them in the words he had learned.

When the lesson was over, he jumped up and hugged the little Bible against his chest.

"I done foun' out! I done foun' out! I done foun' out!" he shouted, his voice high with excitement.

"Found out what, David?" asked Mr. Dan, laughing at his eagerness.

"How to git words out'n this book! Them little black marks, them letters, they makes words! I been so long wantin' to know. An' now I done foun' out," he said again with a happy chuckle.

"Yes, that's the secret, David. I hope before we find your Uncle Hank you'll be able to read your great-grandfather's Bible as well as he could."

The circuit rider tossed a log on the fire and was about to spread the blanket near it when Toppy yelled, "Look out, Mr. Dan! Look out!"

The circuit rider jumped back. Slithering across the dirt floor was a snake a yard long.

Toppy picked up a chunk of wood and smashed its head.

"A pizen copperhead!" he said.

Mr. Dan made sure it was dead with the ax.

"The heat from our fire brought him out," he said. "We had better see if his mate is around."

He took a torch from the fire and held it while Toppy poked into all the corners before they lay down.

"David, you said your *abc*'s in your sleep last night," Mr. Dan told Toppy next morning. "You got as far as *l*, but you left out *g*.

"It is still raining hard," he added. "We may be marooned here for a while longer. There'll be time for another reading lesson."

He took a small book from the saddlebags, one Toppy had not seen before.

"This is Mr. John Wesley's *Primitive Physics — An Easy, Natural Method of Curing Most Diseases*. I want to see what he writes about bites. That copperhead might have bitten one of us last night.

"Here it is: '*Bites* — Squeeze the wound and wash it an hour in salt water — a pound of salt to a quart

60

Toppy smashed its head with a chunk of wood.

of water. Bind salt on the wound for twelve hours.' "

"But we ain't got that much salt," Toppy said seriously.

Mr. Dan laughed. "Then we will have to kill all our snakes before they bite us," he said.

Toppy looked over Mr. Dan's shoulder as he read more "cures."

"Them same little black letters that make words," Toppy said aloud.

"Yes, David, there are many books in our language and every word in every one of them is spelled with the twenty-six letters you are learning. Let's see if you know them in Mr. Wesley's little medicine book."

There was time for another lesson before it stopped raining and they started out again.

CHAPTER SEVEN

Craddock's Crossing

They reached Craddock's Crossing before sundown that afternoon. The circuit rider stopped Big Gray at the first cabin.

"Get down, David, and knock at the door."

"Who are you an' what do you want?" came from a rough voice inside. The door opened and a burley man staggered out to where the circuit rider sat on Big Gray.

"Who are you, I said, an' what's your business?"

Mr. Dan gave Toppy a hand to remount before he answered. "I am a traveling preacher, a minister of the gospel. I will preach tonight in the tavern, against sin and Satan in this settlement."

"Not if Shad Turner gits win' you're here. He done swore he'll shoot the head off'n the next snivelin' preacher that comes to this Crossin'! An' I'm a-goin' atter him, sure's my name's Jeff Martin."

"I will expect you and Shad Turner to hear me to-night," said the preacher as he rode off.

"We'll be thar!" shouted Jeff Martin with an oath.

A woman cracked the door of the next cabin and looked out.

"Howdy, madam," called the circuit rider. "I am Daniel Wilson, a circuit rider. I will preach tonight at the tavern. I hope you will come."

The woman opened the door wide. "I hear-d a sermon wunst, more'n a year ago," she said. "I'd like to hear another one. I'll shore be thar tonight. You better look out fur Shad Turner. He 'lows he'll kill the next preacher who stops at Craddock's Crossin'."

The news traveled ahead. Doors opened, and men, women, and children came out from cabins as the strangers passed.

"We will have a congregation tonight, David," said the circuit rider.

"Let's load the rifle, Mr. Dan," suggested Toppy.

"No, David, I won't need a gun."

"He hain't afeared o' bein' shot at," Toppy said to himself. "I wonder how come."

The tavern was a long hewn-log building with a

broad fireplace at both ends, and small windows covered with paper smeared with bear grease. Sleeping bunks were built against the walls. The circuit rider fastened Big Gray to a hitching post alongside a number of other horses and went inside carrying the saddle and saddlebags. Toppy followed with the blanket roll and ax.

"Can we get food and lodging for ourselves and corn for my horse?" Mr. Dan asked the tavern keeper.

"Might nigh full up," he answered pointing to the two dozen men, women, and children sitting by the two fireplaces. Some of the children were asleep on the floor.

"You seen their horses outside. On the way to Kentuk. Been here two days waitin' fur hit to clear up. Travelin's hard on women and young'uns, but the men folks want to git thar and build their cabins and clear the land 'fore spring plantin' time.

"That there space back o' that table hain't took," he added. "You kin sleep thar fur sixpence each."

The circuit rider handed him two coins and announced, "I will preach in this room tonight."

"A preacher!" said the talkative innkeeper. "I 'lowed so from them clothes you got on. Thar'll be trouble! One o' them travelin' preachers name o' Asbury come 'long bout a year ago. Said some things Shad Turner didn't like. Shad's been sayin' ever since that he 'lows to shoot the next preacher he sees. Most folks is afeard o' Shad. Lives tother side the river. Might not git win' you're here."

"Jeff Martin is going to tell him," the circuit rider told him cheerfully. "By the way," he added, "have you ever known a man by the name of Hank Hall?"

"No, hain't never heered that name afore," answered the little man.

Wonder if we'll fin' 'im, Toppy thought. He almost hoped they wouldn't, not soon anyway.

Before he and Mr. Dan had finished eating the food the tavern keeper brought them on a wooden trencher, the people began to crowd in. Toppy sat on the blanket roll with the rifle on the floor beside him. He watched Mr. Dan mount the sturdy split-log table, Bible and hymnbook in hand, and face his audience — stern-faced, bearded backwoodsmen and tired women with babies in their arms and children clinging to their skirts.

"He hain't study'n 'bout Shad Turner," Toppy said to himself with pride as the preacher began his sermon. "But I wish this here gun was loaded."

Sitting half hidden behind the table he kept looking for Jeff Martin and Shad Turner. Suddenly there was a commotion at the door. The people fell back to make an aisle for a fierce-looking giant with shaggy red hair and beard. Toppy crawled cautiously from behind the table.

The giant stopped, aimed his gun at Daniel Wilson's head and snarled, "We hain't a-goin' to have no more o' that preachin' and prayin'."

Toppy gave a quick spring, hooked his arms around the man's ankles and jerked his feet from under him. As he fell back sprawling on the floor his gun went off, sending the bullet meant for Daniel Wilson through the ceiling.

Some of the men laughed, a woman screamed, and children began to cry. The would-be assassin scrambled to his feet, picked up his empty gun, slunk to the back of the room, and went out the door muttering curses. Jeff Martin followed him.

The preacher began to line out a rousing hymn. "Sing it with me," he urged.

The crowd grew still. A few joined in the singing. Toppy crawled back to his seat on the blanket roll, and Daniel Wilson finished his sermon against sin and Satan. The travelers spread their blankets on the bunks, and the other folks went back to their cabins.

"You probably saved my life, David," whispered the circuit rider when they were bedded down behind the table for the night. "And I think you may have put a stop to Shad Turner's rule in this settlement."

They were wakened before dawn next morning by the travelers on their way to Kentucky.

"We must see them off, David," said Mr. Dan.

Toppy followed him outside, shivering and half asleep. The loud voices of the men and the stamping and snorting of horses soon waked him up. He helped two boys about his age load their baggage on a pack horse, and held a woman's horse while she made herself and her baby comfortable on its back. The circuit rider moved about lending a hand wherever needed. When all were ready, he offered a prayer for their safe journey.

"If ever you come to Kentucky," called a man as the caravan moved off, "thar'll be a place fur you to preach, and a bed fur you to sleep on in our cabin."

After breakfast the circuit rider visited in the cabins, and Toppy chopped wood for the tavern keeper.

"Shad Turner hain't comin' back to preachin' to-night," the little man assured him. "Not atter he wuz tripped up by a young'un like you, missed his mark, and got laughed at. He won't show his face agin, but the preacher better watch out fur 'im and Jeff when you'uns leave. They'll likely follow you."

The tavern was crowded for the night service, and as the tavern keeper had said the two ruffians did not appear.

The circuit rider and Toppy were ready for an early start next morning.

"Mr. Dan, 'fore we go we better had load that gun," Toppy urged.

"No, David, no," the circuit rider said as he slung the rifle over his shoulder. After a pause he added, "I will put my trust in the Lord."

They had not ridden a mile from the settlement when a bullet whizzed over their heads. A second one went through the crown of the circuit rider's hat. He crouched over Big Gray's neck and Toppy crouched over him. The frightened horse plunged down the trail carrying them to safety.

"Another narrow escape," said the circuit rider when they stopped. He took off his hat, looked at the hole through the crown, and felt the top of his head. "Grazed my skull, but did not break the skin."

They rode along in silence the rest of the morning.

Toppy puzzled again over Mr. Dan's fearlessness, so unlike the courage of the quick-triggered men of the mountains.

Is hit the words in the book? he pondered. Mebby when I kin read 'em better, I'll know.

CHAPTER EIGHT

New Friends

By afternoon Toppy was tired and hungry. They had had nothing to eat since breakfast. He was glad when Mr. Dan said, "Let's halt and rest awhile by this stream."

After they had both had a cool drink Mr. Dan asked, "Have you ever used a gun?"

"Pa Brame's gun," answered Toppy, "not a rifle like your'n."

Mr. Dan loaded the rifle and handed it to him.

"See if you can hit that knot on that biggest oak tree."

Toppy took careful aim and hit the knot squarely in the center. When he had done it the second time, the circuit rider showed him how to reload the gun.

"Now go kill a rabbit or a squirrel," he said, "while I make a fire to cook it."

Toppy smiled happily. Another wish come true! He thought of Joady as he walked away with the rifle under his arm. He was about to shoot a squirrel in a tree overhead when a rabbit hopped out of a clump of bushes a yard away. He raised the rifle quickly and fired.

"A good shot!" praised Mr. Dan when Toppy came back holding the rabbit up by its hind legs. "Right through the head! You can be our hunter from now on.

"Skin it," he added, "and wash it in the stream while I rig up a spit. Get the knife from the saddlebags."

Slanted over a bed of coals on a sharp stick thrust at an angle into the ground the rabbit was soon cooking. The good smell made Toppy hungrier and hungrier. He found it hard to wait till it was well done.

"There will be only an hour or two more of daylight," said Mr. Dan when they had eaten the meat from the last bone. "I think we had better camp here tonight. Let's hurry and get our bed made so we will have time for a reading lesson and a story from Granny's Bible."

A light snow fell during the night and laid a white cover over their blanket, keeping them snug and warm.

"A beautiful valley!" said the circuit rider next morning. "And this trail looks as if it has been recently traveled."

73

An hour later Toppy called to him, "We're comin' to a cabin."

"How do you know? I don't see any smoke," said Mr. Dan.

"Don' you hear somebody choppin' on a log?" asked Toppy.

"Yes, I do now," answered the circuit rider. "You have sharp ears, Toppy."

He caught up the slackened rein and urged Big Gray to a faster walk. It was not long before they came to a fresh-made clearing. A man and a boy were working on a two-room cabin. Two horses were tied close by.

"Can we lend a hand?" called the circuit rider. "I am Daniel Wilson, and this is David Hall."

"My name is Stephen Campbell," answered the man. "This is my son Frank. I will be glad to have your help with this roof. The boys can finish the door-step."

As they worked, Frank told David about his mother and sister who were staying in the settlement till their new home was finished.

"I'll stay here and take care things while Pa goes for them. I ain't scared. I'm 'most thirteen. They'll need both horses to hitch to the cart to bring all the fixin's that Ma wouldn't leave behind.

"Ma'll teach me and my sister Jean, since there ain't no school near here."

"School?" asked Toppy.

"Yes," answered Frank. "I went to school to old Mr. McFaddin. More than a dozen of us boys went to his school. I like 'rithmetic and reading but I'm no good at grammar and Latin. I guess I'll go back to Charlotte when I'm old enough and go to Liberty College. That's where Pa went."

Toppy was thinking hard. There were so many things he was finding he did not know.

"Have you always lived in the mountains?" Frank asked. "Are there many bears in the forest?"

Toppy found it easier to answer this friendly boy's questions than to ask questions himself.

"You won't see no bars till the leaves come green agin," he said. "Then they'll come out'n their dens where they been all winter. The she-bar always has one little cub with her, sometimes two.

"Yes, they is mean — the she-bars is — when they has cubs, if'n you bother 'em."

By nightfall the roof was on the cabin. A bright

blaze in the fireplace lighted up the room where a puncheon floor had been laid. Frank brought water from the spring, and Mr. Campbell cooked corn bread and a pheasant he had killed that morning.

"A cup of tea?" he asked. "I brought a bit with me."

This was Toppy's first taste of tea. He did not like it, but Mr. Dan seemed to think it was a treat so he downed his cupful.

"David shot a rabbit for our supper yesterday," said Mr. Dan. "He handles a rifle well."

"You boys might like to shoot at a target after supper," suggested Mr. Campbell. "Frank needs practice."

Toppy was pleased with his new friend's praise as he hit the bull's-eye of the target Mr. Dan tacked on a tree.

Later when the preacher had read the Bible and prayed, the blankets were spread on the floor. Toppy listened as the two men talked. Frank was asleep.

"Do you think Mr. Washington will accept the presidency for another term?" asked the circuit rider.

"The confidence of the whole Union is centered on him," answered Mr. Campbell. "He will accept if he thinks it is his duty."

"A great and God-fearing man," said the circuit rider.

He had told Toppy about President Washington and the national government in Philadelphia.

"Reckon mebby Mr. Washington can git words out lots o' books," Toppy said to himself. "An' Mr. Dan an' Mr. Campbell an' Frank kin. An' I aim to, too." Mr. Campbell, he knew, had bought some of the little books the circuit rider carried in his saddlebags to sell to persons who could read.

Toppy was falling off to sleep when he heard Mr. Campbell say, "You were telling me earlier about David. If you do not find his uncle, bring him back here. We would be glad to have him make his home with us. My wife can teach him with Frank and Jean."

Toppy was wide awake now but he kept his eyes shut and held his breath until Mr. Dan answered.

"I thank you, Mr. Campbell, for David. My territory next year is farther west where the dangers from hostile Indians is great. For this reason I did not dare to suggest at first that he stay with me. But he has proved to be a good companion and an excellent woodsman. So I have almost decided to take him with me if we do not find his father's brother. I have not told him yet."

Toppy was so overjoyed that Mr. Dan was willing to take him on his next circuit that he almost forgot to be grateful for Mr. Campbell's invitation. He found it hard to lie still. "I shore hope we don' ever fin' Granny's boy Hank," he said to himself with his teeth clenched tight.

CHAPTER NINE

Marooned Again

During the next four months Toppy rode with Daniel Wilson over buffalo traces and hatchet-blazed trails to many scattered settlements and lone cabins tucked away in mountain coves. A family was a congregation and a chair or a sawed-off tree trunk served for a pulpit in this thinly populated country. Only one person they asked had ever heard of Hank Hall.

"I knowed Hank," he said, "more'n five years ago. Hain't seen hair nor hide o' him since."

Toppy was always anxious till the question was asked and relieved when the answer was no.

"We have been lucky," the circuit rider said one morning in March. "Snow and rain have stopped us very few times this winter. But it looks now as if we are in for rough weather."

Snow had been falling since daylight. It was coming down so fast Mr. Dan could not see the blazed trees that marked the way. Toppy was glad for the fox skin that covered his knees — a present from their last host. Mr. Dan wrapped his cape closer around his legs and pulled his broad-brimmed hat over his eyes.

"A bad night if we should have to sleep out," he called over his shoulder. "We'll ride on awhile. This fresh-blazed trail must lead somewhere."

Luckily they came to a cabin before dark. Toppy's hands and feet were numb with cold. His stomach felt empty. How good the fire looked when the cabin door opened! And the odor of roasting meat, and corn pones cooking! He stood rubbing his cold hands together and sniffing the delightful smells. From the split-log fireboard a chunk of venison haunch hung suspended on a stout vine. As it swung in front of the hot fire, the drippings from it sputtered into a wooden trencher on the hearth.

When Toppy saw that there were six children and three grown-ups in the family besides Mr. Dan and himself, he wondered if the food would go round. He was relieved when one of the women mixed more corn bread and filled a second skillet.

When they were bedded down for the night, Toppy found himself in the loft alongside the three boys in the family. He thought of Joady, Buddy, and Ronny.

"I wish I could see 'em. I wish Joady could shoot Mr. Dan's rifle. And I wish Buddy and Ronny could ride Big Gray some."

A whiff of smoked bear meat hanging from the rafters over his head made Toppy think of the cinnamon bear that he and Joady had found the day they were gathering chestnuts. He went to sleep and dreamed he was in the cabin on Thicketty Mountain.

"Snowed in, looks like. Can't git the door open 'count o' the snow piled 'ginst it," said their host next morning. "Good we got plenty corn, and meat hanging in the loft."

Toppy knew what this meant. Outside snow and ice, inside eleven people cooped up together for two, maybe three or four days. He remembered Ma Brame's fire stick and Pa Brame's rawhide strap at times like this back on Thicketty Mountain.

"Let's open the door and get a path dug to the woodpile," said the circuit rider, "before the snow gets any deeper."

The two men put their shoulders against the door

and pushed till there was a crack big enough to slip through. With a crude shovel they made the path.

Mr. Dan and Toppy helped to keep it cleared all day. Between times, with a child on each knee and the others nearby, the circuit rider told stories and he and Toppy sang together.

"We will all sit back," Mr. Dan had suggested, "and give the women folks room to cook at the hearth."

Somehow the cabin did not seem as crowded to Toppy as the Thicketty Mountain cabin had been. He counted the members of the family again. "Nine, 'sides the dog. An' me an' Mr. Dan makes 'leven. We was jist nine 't th' Brames.' "

During the long afternoon the circuit rider taught them all to play a game with grains of corn, and to sing hymns as he lined them out. Toppy enjoyed the game and the singing as much as his young hosts did.

"David, show Martha and Buck and Jesse the words in Granny's Bible and teach them their *abc*'s," said Mr. Dan when they had all learned to say the Lord's Prayer by heart.

This was a proud moment for Toppy. He felt as important as he had the first time he used Mr. Dan's rifle.

With a child on each knee, the circuit rider told stories.

"There are twenty-six letters," he said, talking as much like the circuit rider as he could. "Twenty-two of 'em are in this prayer. Say 'em with me as I touch 'em with this splinter."

Martha was an apt pupil. After a second lesson she became as eager to learn to read as Toppy himself had been.

"I reckon mebby you kin someday," Toppy told her, "if'n you jist keep on a-wishin'."

A heavy rain the fourth night washed away most of the snow. The trail was clear, and the sun shone bright.

The circuit rider took a small book from the saddle-bags, one that Toppy had read through twice. "You can give this to Martha, David," he said.

Toppy opened the little book and put it in her hands.

"Marthy," he said, "you might kin learn yourself to read out this here. All them letters I learnt you is in hit."

Martha thanked him with a broad smile and shining eyes.

CHAPTER TEN

Springtime

Another month passed and there was not a trace of snow except on the tops of the highest peaks. The nights were still cold but the days were warm and sunny.

"This April weather is more like May," said the circuit rider. "Spring is just around the corner."

"I hear-d a redbird a-whistlin' jist now," said Toppy.

"Yes, I heard him too, a cardinal," said Mr. Dan. "And listen! That's a Carolina wren."

"A leetle bit a bird with hardly no tail feathers?" asked Toppy.

"Yes. You must learn the right names of all the birds you know so well by sight and sound. Many of them tell us their name by color or song — blue bird, bobwhite, whippoorwill, redheaded woodpecker."

Toppy was in a talkative mood. He told Mr. Dan about the bobwhite nest he found from which he and Joady got seventeen eggs. He described mud-lined nests that were built every year in the same tree. And finally he asked, "What are 'em pretty birds that eats the little buds of'n the trees? They sits right still — don' sing none — a whole passel of 'em on one limb."

"Robins build the mud-lined nests," Mr. Dan told him. "And the pretty, silent birds are cedar waxwings. Cherry birds we called them because they ate all our cherries in the spring."

That night they lay on a pine-bough bed under a starry sky.

"You know where to look for the Big Dipper, David, and the North Star," said Mr. Dan. "Follow the two top stars of the Dipper to the right till you come to a big reddish-yellow star. Do you see it? The name is Arcturus. There are millions of stars in the heavens, but only a few are named. Arcturus is mentioned in the Bible."

"Thar's Orion, too, way down thar. Hit was up thar when you first showed hit to me," said Toppy.

Toppy drank in all the circuit rider taught him day after day. And the more he learned, the greater was his eagerness to know more. Lessons in Granny's Bible were irregular, but memorizing and spelling and singing went on hour after hour as they traveled lonely trails. Big Gray's back was their classroom. Often Mr. Dan would read aloud, his book in one hand and the reins in the other. It was easy now for Toppy to ask questions, and the circuit rider always seemed able to answer them.

"The latch is on the outside this time, David," he said one afternoon when he stopped Big Gray before a cabin with a newly felled tree in the yard.

Toppy knew that this meant food and shelter. They had passed a cabin the day before where the latchstring was not on the outside. Gruff voices had cursed them and ordered them to move on. This time a young woman with a child on her hip opened the door.

"Come in," she said. "Nobody here cep'n me and this little young'un and my man. An' him not able to walk."

They found her husband lying on a pile of skins by the fire.

"Can't git up," he said. "Slipped cuttin' down a tree and hurted this leg."

"Let's have a look at it," said the circuit rider.

The woman put the child in its wooden cradle and threw pine cones on the fire for a better light.

"A break," said the circuit rider when he had examined the leg. "Not a bad one. I think I can fix it."

He picked up a thin slab of wood by the chimney. "David, split this and trim both sides smooth with the ax."

While Toppy trimmed the soft white pine, the circuit rider took his clean homespun shirt from the saddlebags and tore it into strips. He gave one piece to the woman.

"Wet this," he said, "and bathe his face. David, you will have to hold the ends of the bones together — like this."

Toppy took hold and watched Mr. Dan bind the splints to the broken limb. The man's face was drawn with pain but he made no sound. Toppy's breathing was fast but his hands were as steady as Mr. Dan's.

The cabin had a dirt floor, the usual mud-daubed chimney, and a table, a stool, and a bench all made of split logs. Forked sticks driven into the earth held a rough frame covered with skins. When the woman had given them food and water to drink, the man pointed to the bed.

"You two kin turn in over thar," he insisted. "Me
and her kin sleep right here."

The circuit rider would not hear to this arrange-
ment. "David and I will feel more at home on the
floor," he said.

"Easy now," he warned as they lifted the man to
the bed.

"Young bones heal quickly," the circuit rider told the man next day, "but you had better stay off that leg for a while. David and I will kill a rabbit and a squirrel or two, and finish chopping that tree into fire wood."

"That shore'll be kind-thoughted o' you," said the woman.

Later the little girl crawled out of the cabin door and toddled over to where the circuit rider and Toppy were stacking the wood. She laughed aloud when Mr. Dan tossed her up in the air. Toppy cut the tail off one of the squirrels he had killed and put it in her hand.

"Here's a play-pretty fur you," he said.

The child was shy again and toddled back to the cabin.

Before they left next morning the circuit rider eased the bandage on the man's leg and warned him again about trying to walk too soon.

CHAPTER ELEVEN

"Good Work, David"

During the long summer months Daniel Wilson and Toppy made a third and a fourth round of the circuit that was three hundred miles in circumference. There was always a welcome on the return visits. The children would come running, but stop before they reached Big Gray and peer from behind a laurel thicket.

"Take them to ride, David, while I visit around and make ready to preach tonight," the circuit rider would say.

New families were moving in. But inquiries still brought no news of Hank Hall. Toppy felt almost sure now that they would not find his uncle.

"We must go by Caleb Smith's cabin and see how that family is getting on since our last visit," the circuit rider said one morning.

Mrs. Smith was standing in the door as they rode up, three towheaded children peeping from behind her skirts.

"Hear-d you singin'," she said. "Knowed hit was you'uns. Light and come in. My man hain't here. Went huntin' mos' a week ago. Lookin' fur him back mos' any time. I got corn meal. I'll bake you a pone."

Toppy added the food that was in the saddlebags to the lunch, and brought water from the spring.

"Now you young'uns git outdoors," said the mother when they had eaten.

The oldest, a tousled-haired wisp of a girl, obeyed. The others still clung to their mother's skirts and stared at the strangers.

"I'm shore glad to have somebody to talk to 'sides chaps," said Mrs. Smith.

The circuit rider sat on the slab bench and listened to her troubles before he read the Bible and prayed.

"David," he said, looking at his watch, "load the rifle and kill some game before we leave. I'll stir up this fire and chop some wood. Caleb may not get back today."

"Now that's kind-thoughted o' you'uns," said Mrs. Smith.

When Toppy stepped out the door, the sight that met his eyes brought the loaded gun quickly to his shoulder. No time to call for help! The little tousled-haired girl was playing at the edge of the clearing, and not three yards from her a panther crouched lashing his long, thick tail ready to spring.

One shot killed him!

The mother screamed as she rushed to her child and grabbed her up in her arms. Mr. Dan stood looking at the limp beast on the ground, his hand on Toppy's shoulder. "Good work, David," he whispered.

The woman took her children into the house, and the circuit rider and Toppy dragged the dead panther up the mountain side and pushed it over the edge of a cliff.

"David, you chop the wood," Mr. Dan said. "I'll get a rabbit or a few squirrels."

Caleb Smith did come home just as they were ready to leave. When he learned what had happened, he caught Toppy's arm in an iron grip.

"Stay and eat," he urged pointing to the pile of game he had dropped on the ground.

When the circuit rider said they could not stay this time, Caleb tied the legs of a brace of partridges and a pheasant together with a vine and hung them on the pommel of the saddle.

That night on their pine-bough bed Toppy lay thinking about the little Smith girl and the hungry beast that would have killed her.

"David," Mr. Dan had said, "your sure aim and quick action this afternoon saved a little child's life.

We should be thankful for your skill in handling a rifle."

Praise from Mr. Dan always made Toppy glad. He recalled the first night that he had slept under the stars with the circuit rider. So much had happened since! The visit from the Indians; the fire at River Bend; setting the man's broken leg.

"And I kin read! All by myself I kin git words out Granny's pa's Bible." He smiled as he said it over and over to himself, "I kin read! I kin read! Like Mr. Dan and the Killians and Mr. Campbell and Frank.

"Looks like we hain't goin' to fin' my uncle Hank. An' Mr. Dan'll take me with him crost the mountains. Wonder what hit'll be like over thar?"

It was a long time before he went to sleep.

CHAPTER TWELVE

Lost

One sunny afternoon when they had left the last settlement on the last round of the circuit, they stopped to make camp near a spring on the side of the mountain.

"October again," said Mr. Dan. "Just one year, David, since Pa Brame lifted you up behind me on Big Gray's back. You have grown taller. A good companion you've been these twelve months. Are you still glad you came?"

Toppy answered with his slow, shy smile that still sometimes took the place of words. After a moment he said, "You knowed the answer to that before you ast me."

Daniel Wilson laughed. "I think I will climb to the top of this mountain and see if I see smoke coming from any chimneys in the next valley.

"Start a fire and make our bed," he added, as he picked up his gun. "My legs need stretching. I'll bring back a couple of squirrels or a rabbit for supper. I won't be gone long."

Toppy got busy right away chopping wood and pine boughs. He felt proud that Mr. Dan trusted him to do it all alone. It was the first time. As he worked he sang the hymn he liked best of all the ones he had learned to sing with the circuit rider:

"We want no cowards in our band,
Who will our colors fly,
But call for valient-hearted men
Who are not afraid to die."

When the bed had been made and plenty of wood cut for the night, he led Big Gray to a nearby stream for water. He fastened the bridle to an overhanging limb and took the curry-comb from the saddlebags. Carefully he combed the shaggy coat, lifted each foot to see if a pebble might be lodged in a hoof, and picked the cockleburs from the thick black tail. Big Gray nuzzled his shoulder and made little noises in his nose.

"Oh, Mr. Dan lef' the shot bag!" Toppy said aloud, noticing the bag at the foot of a tree. "That means no squirrels or rabbit."

In a nearby cedar tree there were passenger pigeons so tame he could almost reach up and lift them from their perch.

"We'll have pigeons for supper 'stead of squirrels or rabbit."

He killed two with a stick and got them ready for roasting. He remembered that Mr. Dan had said a good woodsman kills only what game he needs for food. But it was no temptation to him to keep on killing these beautiful gray birds with their long graceful bodies.

When everything was in readiness for the night, he opened Mr. John Wesley's little medicine book in which he had had several reading lessons.

When he had read the "cure" for cuts and bruises and for chills and fever, he leaned back against a tree with the medicine book on his lap.

"Wonder if I could be a doctor like Mr. Dan's brother when I'm a growed-up man?" He played with the idea several minutes.

"Better get these birds cooked," he said as he jumped to his feet and put the medicine book back in the saddlebags.

On a spit rigged on two forked sticks he roasted

the pigeons to a golden brown, and laid them near the fire on a piece of pine bark.

The sun was easing down to the horizon and Mr. Dan had not come back. Toppy began to feel uneasy.

He's been gone a long time, he was thinking.

When the sun sank out of sight and the darkness crowded in on him, he became alarmed. He piled more wood on the fire, but the blaze only emphasized the blackness of the night.

"Mr. Dan! Mr. Dan! Mr. Dan!" he called.

There was no answer but the echo of his own frightened voice. Again and again and again he called, each time more frantically. Big Gray seemed to sense that something was wrong and began to whinny and paw the ground with a heavy hoof. Toppy put his arms around the horse's neck.

"Big Gray. Oh, Big Gray, what kin we do? What kin we do?"

"Please, God, don' let 'im be lost. Please, God," he prayed with his face against Big Gray's side.

He snatched a blazing brand from the fire and waved it above his head. "Come back, Mr. Dan! Come back! Come back!"

Louder and louder he shouted, going up the moun-

"Mr. Dan! Mr. Dan! Here we are! Here we are!"

tain side as far from the fire as he dared. He stopped and listened. What he heard was not an echo, not the familiar night calls of the forest creatures. Faint, but unmistakable, he heard it again.

"Keep calling, David! Keep calling!"

Joy took the place of terror in Toppy's voice. "Mr. Dan! Mr. Dan! Here we are! Here we are!"

Closer and closer the answer came back, "Keep calling, David, keep calling."

Following the sound of Toppy's voice the circuit rider finally came stumbling through the underbrush. He caught Toppy in his arms and held him close for a moment. Neither spoke as they walked to the fire and sat down. Mr. Dan's face and hands were scratched and his clothes were torn. Toppy brought him a drink of water in the pewter cup.

"Better than squirrel or rabbit," the circuit rider said when they were eating the pigeons with a handful of roasted corn. And looking at the fire and the hemlock bed he added, "You are a good woodsman, David. A better one than I am. I am sure now that I will take you with me when I go west if we do not find your uncle before I leave."

Toppy's joy was too great to put into words.

"I did see smoke from chimneys in the valley," Mr. Dan went on. "Looked like quite a settlement at the far end. We will ride down in the morning and see who keeps those fires burning."

They were silent for a long time as they lay on the pine-bough bed under the sky. Toppy was so still the circuit rider might have thought he was asleep. But suddenly he sat up and said, "Mr. Dan, I aim to be a Christian like you an' Mr. Killian an' Miz. Killian an' ole Uncle Sol."

"I am glad, David. I was about your age when I became a Christian and joined the church. I have never been sorry."

"When kin I join?" Toppy asked.

"The next time I give the invitation. You have heard it many times."

CHAPTER THIRTEEN

Rattlesnake Cove

Next morning they rode over the mountain and stopped by a clear, winding creek. There in the quiet sunny valley between tree-covered peaks the circuit rider baptized Toppy. Together they knelt beside the mountain stream and prayed the Lord's Prayer.

Later in the day they met a hunter and asked him about the distance to the settlement Mr. Dan had seen from the mountaintop.

"Rattlesnake Cove hit's called. Hain't more'n two miles as the crow flies," said the hunter. "Six by trail. You kin ride up the creek at tother en'."

When they had ridden four or five miles, Mr. Dan headed Big Gray into the shallow water. "Here's where we can travel upstream," he said.

Sure-footed Big Gray picked his way carefully over the rocky creek bed. The circuit rider began to sing and Toppy joined in. They were still singing when they left the stream and rode into the settlement. A crowd had gathered and a strapping fellow came to meet them with a horsewhip in his hand.

"We don' need none o' yo singin'," he roared. "Git out 'o here, and be on yo way!"

He gave Big Gray a resounding whack with his whip. The startled horse, unaccustomed to blows, reared on his hind legs. Toppy taken unawares, landed on the ground. When he had quieted Big Gray, Daniel Wilson sprang from the saddle and handed the rein to Toppy who had picked himself up unhurt. Quick as a flash the circuit rider snatched the whip from the man's hand and threw it as far as he could send it. The crowd laughed, and the ruffian muttered curses.

The circuit rider turned his back on him and asked in a friendly voice, "Is there a blacksmith in Rattlesnake Cove? My horse needs shoeing. I'll pay nine pence — the usual charge."

A man with powerful arms and shoulders but a twisted foot limped forward and took hold of Big Gray's bridle.

"I'll shoe your mount. Come eat first, you and the boy."

He tied Big Gray in front of his rude log smithy and led the way to his cabin. It was piled to the rafters with pelts.

"My name is Rush. Patrick Rush. 'Pa Rush' ever'-body calls me, bein' as how I am the oldest settler in these parts," he told them. "Can't hunt no more 'count o' this foot, so I blacksmiths. My two boys is the best trappers in these hills. They ain't comin' home till next week so there's plenty room and plenty skins to sleep on if you aimin' to stay awhile."

"Thank you, Pa Rush," said the circuit rider. "David, bring in the blanket roll; I'll get the saddle."

They shared Pa Rush's meal of venison and bear meat. Toppy looked on with wonder and admiration the next morning as Pa Rush heated four curved irons in the forge till they were soft, hammered them on the anvil, and dipped them in a tub of water. He heated, hammered, and dipped till they were the proper shape. Then he put the new shoes on Big Gray's heavy hoofs.

They spent three days in Rattlesnake Cove. The circuit rider preached morning, afternoon, and night. A sawed-off tree trunk was his pulpit. In between times he visited in the cabins while Toppy took the children to ride on Big Gray. At night they both listened to Pa Rush's tales of buffalo hunts and Indian raids.

"Did you ever meet a man by the name of Hank Hall in your travels?" the circuit rider asked him.

"Yes, I knowed Big Hank Hall. Best shot in these parts. Little more'n a year ago he wuz huntin' with my boys. Took sick one day and died. They buried him near the tradin' pos' on Mud Creek. This here powder horn wuz his'n."

Toppy took the powder horn in his hand. He thought of Granny, and his father whom he could not remember, and the uncle whom he had seen only twice. "I'm the only Hall left now," he said to himself.

Sam Pitts did not show his face at the preaching till the afternoon of the last day. With him were two loud, rough men. Their presence did not seem to bother Mr. Dan, but Toppy was a bit uneasy.

Halfway through the service Sam Pitts sneaked over, caught Toppy by his collar, reached for a stick, and raised it to strike.

"Give 'im the beatin' ye promised the preacher," yelled one of his companions.

In three strides Daniel Wilson reached them, grabbed the stick, and raised his arm threatingly. He stood for a full minute — his eyes blazing, his breath

coming hard — one hundred and eighty pounds of bone and muscle. The bully let go of Toppy's collar, cowered, and swore.

"Wallup 'im, preacher, wallup 'im good," called Pa Rush.

Slowly the circuit rider lowered his arm, dropped the stick on the ground, walked back to the stump, and continued his sermon. A few minutes later a rock struck his cheek. He wiped the blood off with the back of his hand and preached on.

The crowd was silent. Toppy's face flushed, but he unclenched his fists and took a deep breath. He was beginning to understand Mr. Dan's fearlessness.

"It's 'cause he knows about God," he said to himself.

At the night service he sat on a log with Pa Rush near the fire. He looked around for Sam Pitts and his crowd.

"Don' you worry. Them rascals hain't comin'!" Pa Rush whispered.

Toppy had on a new coonskin cap the old man had made for him with a fluffy tail dangling down behind.

"Ole Mam Jinny's makin' you a new jacket, too, out'n one o' my bes' buckskins, wid two big pockets like the preacher tole her to, an' new breeches. Be done 'fore you leave," Pa Rush said.

After the sermon came the invitation Toppy was expecting. The circuit rider stood inside the altar — two heavy pine logs laid end to end. When Toppy started forward, Pa Rush put a hand on his shoulder and limped along beside him. Daniel Wilson reached for Toppy's hand with his right and Patrick Rush's with his left and held them in a firm grip.

Half the crowd joined them at the altar. A light snow was falling when the circuit rider began to sing *Forth in Thy Name, O Lord, I Go*. The congregation took it up and sang as they went back to their homes.

Pa Rush closed the door of the cabin when they were inside and spread skins on the bunks against the wall. Toppy sat by the fire, his chin in his hands, thinking, while the circuit rider checked the contents of the saddlebags.

"Yes, like I tole you, Hank Hall is dead," said Pa Rush. "But you kin leave this boy with me. I'll learn him to be a blacksmith."

Toppy smiled his thanks.

"David appreciates your invitation, Pa Rush," the circuit rider told him. "But I guess I'll be taking him along with me.

"Let's get a good night's sleep, David. I have a plan I'll tell you about tomorrow."

CHAPTER FOURTEEN

Salisbury Town

The circuit rider and Pa Rush were standing by the door talking when Toppy waked up next morning.

"Take the trail over yon mountains down tother side through Chinquapin Gap," Pa Rush was saying. "You'll hit the road goin' clean to Salisbury town."

Toppy jumped out of the bunk and joined them.

"I used to trade my pelts in Salisbury town," the old man went on. "Aim to go again some day. My boys goes ever' year. Big town they say. Fine houses. Lots o' rich folks."

"Yes," answered Mr. Dan. "I was in Salisbury two years ago. It is a growing town."

He turned to Toppy. "How would you like to ride over to Salisbury, David, and on to Baltimore?"

Toppy drew in a deep breath through his mouth and stood speechless with surprise.

"I've told you about my doctor brother in Baltimore," said Mr. Dan, "whom I have not seen in more than three years. He's my only kin in America. I'd like to pay him a visit. And while there we can refill the saddlebags with reading matter."

Toppy recovered his voice. "Goin' down the mountains like Granny reckoned mebby I would? Goin' to see what's on tother side like she said I mebby might when I wuz a grown-up man?"

"You are not going to have to wait till you are grown," Mr. Dan said.

Toppy was too excited to eat his breakfast.

"How fur is it, Mr. Dan? How long 'll it take to git thar? How long'll we stay?"

In his eagerness he forgot to say *get* and *there* as he was trying hard to do.

The circuit rider answered his questions as they saddled Big Gray. Pa Rush gave them further directions, advice, and food before they left.

By noon they had passed through Chinquapin Gap and were on a narrow road leading to the east. Tall trees walled them in on both sides and shut out the sun. Overhanging branches brushed the top of the circuit rider's hat. Deep ruts, rocks, stumps, and mud as sticky as glue made traveling slow and difficult.

It was not long before they came to a stalled ox-drawn wagon.

"Kin you help us?" called the driver.

"Hop down, David," said Mr. Dan. "Take the ax and begin to cut boughs to lay in the ruts. I'll hitch Big Grap to the wagon tongue."

While they were working, two Indians came along with a horse dragging poles on which were loaded a pile of skins. They were friendly and talkative and willing to lend a hand. Toppy watched them with interest and curiosity. This was only the second time he had been close to the men he had been taught to fear.

"Most of the Indians we will see from now on will be friendly," Mr. Dan told him.

Later that afternoon they passed another wagon and a heavy two-wheeled cart, both drawn by slow, straining oxen. The circuit rider stopped Big Gray and talked to the weary travelers. Toppy looked back as long as he could see them, wondering about the boy and girl who peered at him from the back of the wagon.

"We will stay here tonight," Mr. Dan said when

they came to a village. Twenty or more families lived in three and four room hewn-log cabins and two-story frame houses. The dwellings were clustered around a courthouse and a log meetinghouse.

The next day was Sunday. Toppy sat on the front split-log bench and for the first time heard the circuit rider preach from a pulpit to a congregation seated in a meetinghouse.

"Will Salisbury be bigger than this town?" Toppy asked Mr. Dan.

"Yes, it's quite a bit bigger," answered the circuit rider.

The next night found them only a few miles from Salisbury.

"There's a full moon," said Mr. Dan. "We can see to ride on."

Toppy was leaning heavily against the circuit rider's broad back when they arrived and found a bed at Boar's Head Inn. On the huge sign over the door was a picture of George Washington.

The three days spent in Salisbury were filled with new sights and new experiences for Toppy. The third morning a stagecoach driven at full speed stopped at the tavern door. A crowd gathered to watch as the

driver jerked the four exhausted horses to a stop. Two grooms quickly hitched fresh horses to the coach while the footman helped half a dozen passengers off with their baggage and loaded as many more.

"I'd shore like to ride in that thing," Toppy said as the driver caught up the reins, cracked his long whip, and was off again.

"You probably will ride in a stagecoach some day," said Mr. Dan, "but you won't find it much more comfortable than Big Gray's back."

"Oh, I'd rather ride Big Gray," said Toppy quickly.

He looked around at the horses, oxen, covered wagons, carts, carriages, and people. People everywhere! Toppy had never dreamed there were so many people in the world. Men in broadcloth knee breeches, satin vests, and cocked hats. Men in velvet, in buckskins, and in ragged tow cloth. Indians with tomahawks in their belts. Black people with bundles on their heads. Ladies riding in two-wheeled carriages, holding fancy parasols over their fashionable bonnets.

Toppy stood still and stared. "Mr. Dan, Baltimore can't be no bigger'n Salisbury!"

Mr. Dan laughed. "Oh, yes, a good deal bigger, David. Roads from the west and the great Catawba Trading Path from South Carolina to Pennsylvania meet here in Salisbury. Many people pass through. The Trading Path is one of the oldest roads in the country. We will take it in the morning when we start to Baltimore."

The same crowd that gathered to see the stagecoach was there later to see the post rider on his weather-stained horse. He brought the mail from Charleston and soon set out again with a letter Daniel Wilson had written to his brother in Baltimore. Toppy had watched the circuit rider write it with quill pen and ink borrowed from the innkeeper.

Late in the afternoon a fleet of four covered wagons each drawn by six powerful horses with bells on their bridles drew up near the inn.

Toppy and Mr. Dan watched the drivers unhitch their horses and tie them, three on each side, to the long wagon tongues, to eat from troughs placed between.

"Horses look like Big Gray," commented Toppy.

"Same powerful breed," said Mr. Dan. "They are hauling freight, fine furniture, and tools that came over in ships from England to Charleston."

Toppy had seen so much that day he was ready for bed at sundown.

CHAPTER FIFTEEN

Toppy's Decision

The journey from Salisbury to Baltimore took more than two weeks. The late October days were fair and cool, and Big Gray carried them along at a steady pace.

"Twenty-five, Mr. Dan!" called Toppy one morning. They had caught up with and passed a train of pack horses tied head to tail, carrying furs and hides to market. "The last one jist had seventeen."

Next he was counting the long, boat-shape covered wagons, traveling north and south, drawn by plodding oxen. The much traveled Trading Path was barely wide enough for two of the wagons to pass each other.

"Pioneer families in most of them," said Mr. Dan, "on their way to new homes. This is the road your Granny and her pa and ma came down, David, when she was a little baby."

"Granny'd be proud if she knowed where I'm gwine — goin'," said Toppy.

The most exciting event of the journey for Toppy was a visit with three families who had stopped their wagons by the roadside.

"Tomorrow is Sunday," one of the men explained when the circuit rider drew rein and greeted him. "We do not travel on the Sabbath."

"Nor do we," said the circuit rider.

Toppy was glad when he heard him accept the man's invitation to tarry with them till Monday.

After supper and prayers their host announced, "The preacher will sleep in my wagon."

"Let David sleep in ours," begged Mac and Mark, twin boys a year or two younger than Toppy.

"I think we can make room," said their mother.

"Now I'll get to see inside one o' them big wagons!" Toppy said to himself.

The circuit rider preached twice on Sunday to the three families as they gathered about the campfire. By Monday morning Toppy had gotten acquainted with more boys and girls than he had ever known before.

Two days later he and Mr. Dan were riding over cobblestones on a narrow street in Baltimore. Mr. Dan stopped Big Gray at one of the neat brick houses that lined both sides of the street and tied him to the hitching post.

Out of the front door came an elderly man with outstretched hand. "Dan, Dan, I am glad to see you."

"And I am just as glad to see you, Andy."

"I got your letter," said Dr. Wilson, "only an hour ago. I hardly expected you so soon.

"And this is David. Welcome, my boy, welcome! Come right in both of you. Zeke will come get your horse and bring in your saddlebags, Dan."

He looks like Mr. Dan. He's not as big, but he's lots older, Toppy decided as they followed Andrew Wilson into a small room that served as his living room and office.

"I will tell my housekeeper to put two more plates on the table, and we will have dinner. I know David is hungry."

During the next few days Mr. Dan took Toppy sightseeing when the Doctor was making his rounds.

"Where shall we go first today?" Mr. Dan would ask.

Toppy's answer was always, "To the harbor!"

He never tired of watching the loading and unloading of the big boats with the great white sails.

On Sunday the circuit rider was invited to preach in the church his brother attended. After the service Toppy and Mr. Dan stood at the door with Dr. Wilson. Dr. Wilson introduced them both to the people who came past. He introduced one old gentleman in black broadcloth and ruffled shirt as Anthony Wainwright.

"And this is my brother's young friend, David Hall," the doctor finished.

"David *Wainwright* Hall, by the way, sir," added Mr. Dan.

Anthony Wainwright stared at Toppy. "David Wainwright? Who are you, boy? Where did you come from?" he asked in a whisper.

"I come from Thicketty Mountain, sir."

"Where did you get that name?"

Toppy took Granny's Bible from his pocket, turned to the fly-leaf, and handed it to Mr. Wainwright.

"My brother's Bible!" the man exclaimed. "My brother David who left Bristol for the colonies when I was seven years old. The last letter we had from him he was on his way from Pennsylvania to the Carolinas with his wife and infant daughter. When I was twenty,

I came to America to find him. I went to the Carolinas, but found no trace of him.

"Where did you get this Bible, David?"

"It was Granny's pa's, sir. And she said he could get the words out o' it," Toppy answered.

"David's grandmother died more than a year ago," explained the circuit rider. "He has been with me ever since."

"She must have been the little daughter about whom my brother wrote us," said Anthony Wainwright.

He continued to stare at Toppy. "Tall, slight of build, Wainwright eyes," he said.

"Just like your own, sir," said Dr. Wilson. "The likeness is striking."

"Come with me, David, and Brother Wilson, and you too, Dr. Wilson," urged Mr. Wainwright. "I must tell my wife the good news right away! My carriage is outside."

Toppy's first ride in a carriage! Drawn by two spanking chestnut roans.

"Praise de Lawd!" said Uncle Isaac, the old driver when Mr. Wainwright told him who Toppy was. "He shore do be a Wainwright, wid dem same blue eyes. Jist lak young Marse Tony's wuz, aint dey? An' tall, too, lak him."

"My son Anthony was killed in our country's fight for freedom," explained Mr. Wainwright.

"So was David's father. In the Battle of King's Mountain," said the circuit rider.

Uncle Isaac stopped the carriage in front of an imposing three-story brick house. Mr. Wainwright began calling as he opened the front door. "Beth, Bethie, where are you? I have found Brother David's great grandson! He has my brother's Bible with his name in it! And the boy's name is David, too!"

The loveliest lady Toppy had ever seen came down the wide hall. She shook hands with the circuit rider and Dr. Wilson while her husband told her about David.

"Then I am your Aunt Beth," she said with a smile that made little crinkles round her eyes.

"There is much to talk about," said Mr. Wainwright, "but we will have dinner first."

"Brother Wilson," he said as they talked together in the drawing room after dinner, "I recognize your claim on David. I can see how much you mean to each other. But I would like to keep him and send him to Cokesbury College."

"'I think so much of him," answered Daniel Wilson slowly, "that I would not stand in his way. This opportunity, sir, seems providential. I went to Cokesbury, and I would like him to go there, too. But we will leave the decision to him."

Toppy was silent. He could hardly believe his ears. He looked from one to the other. Leave Mr. Dan and Big Gray? "No, no!" he said to himself. "Mr. Dan done promised to take me with 'im if we didn't fin' Granny's boy Hank."

"To have you here, David, during your holidays would mean much to your Aunt Beth and me. We have been lonesome since our Anthony went away."

Toppy still sat silent and tense. It was Aunt Beth who suggested that he wait a day or two before he decided.

"You don't know us very well yet," she said.

"We will ride down to Abingdon, where Cokesbury is located, tomorrow," said Uncle Anthony. "It is only twenty-five miles from Baltimore. Then you can see for yourself, David, if you want to study there."

After a long pause he added, "And, my boy, I want you to know that when I came to America I brought with me my brother's share of our father's estate — one hundred pounds. I invested it in my ship-building business and today it is worth perhaps eight thousand dollars. This is yours, David, whether you stay or go."

"Eight thousand dollars!" Toppy gasped. He had never in his whole life owned as much as a sixpence. The sum was overwhelming.

"I — I — I can't — I don'," he stammered. "I don' need it."

Then slowly he rose from his chair and stood straight and tall, looking older than his twelve and a half years.

"Uncle Anthony, I won't have no use for all that money." His voice was steady now and very serious. "You see I aim to be a circuit rider when I'm a grown-up man."

"God's blessing on you, my boy," said his uncle.

There was silence in the room for several minutes before Daniel Wilson cleared his throat and said quietly, "If you are going to preach, David, you must get ready. Your uncle is offering you the opportunity to do this. The question of your great-grandfather's money can wait."

The next day was cold but fair, and the post road to Abingdon was one of the best in the country. Toppy rode a beautiful young sorrel named Jewel.

"She gentle, but she got sperrit, too," Uncle Isaac said as he adjusted the stirrups of the saddle that had been young Anthony's.

At Abingdon an elderly professor showed them over the college. "We teach ancient languages, agriculture, morals, and religion," he said, "besides all the English branches."

Toppy was impressed, but had no idea what it all meant.

"There are the rules of our college," the professor went on, pointing to the printed list on the wall. Toppy read the list eagerly.

> In bed before nine at night.
> Out of bed before five in the morning.
> Seven hours' study daily.
> Work and recreation daily out of doors —
>   gardening, walking, and riding.
> No feather beds.

To a boy who had slept on a bearskin in a cabin loft most of his life the last rule suggested no hardship. And seven hours' study daily? Toppy had seen the library with rows of books on shelves reaching half-way to the ceiling. Seven hours would not be enough to get the words out of all of them he thought.

They stood on the steps of the building and looked up the Susquehanna Valley and down to the sea.

"Mr. Dan! Mr. Dan!" Toppy's voice was husky with excitement. "Would Granny's pa's money build a school on Thicketty Mountain — with a room full o' books — so Joady an' Buddy an' Ronny an' the Pickett boys an' Marthy an' — "

"It would, David, it would! On Thicketty Mountain or somewhere nearby," interrupted the circuit rider equally excited.

A bell was calling them to supper. Toppy looked at the seventy students at the tables. Several of them were no older than he was. Would he soon be one of them? He had not quite made up his mind.

The next morning on the way back to Baltimore as Jewel cantered alongside Big Gray and Uncle Anthony's chestnut roan, Toppy tried to come to a decision. The books in the library; the sea as he had seen it from the college steps; Uncle Anthony and Aunt Beth; Jewel (Uncle Anthony had said she would be his); and the room with the wide fireplace, glass windows, and huge feather bed.

All these he weighed against being with Mr. Dan on Big Gray's back; riding over hatchet-blazed trails and buffalo traces, sleeping on hemlock boughs under the stars or on bearskins in a log cabin; killing wild game and cooking it over hot coals; singing and spelling and reading and long talks. He smiled as he recalled that first reading lesson when they were marooned in the hunter's shack and he killed the copperhead with a chunk of wood.

He thought about Granny. "She'd want me to stay, and Mr. Dan does."

When they were back in Baltimore at his uncle's front door, he dismounted and gave Jewel's reins to Uncle Isaac. Standing on the stoop he looked at the circuit rider who was just getting off of Big Gray. Hot tears stung his eyelids as he thought of them riding off without him. Aunt Beth opened the door and they all went into the living room. Toppy stood by his chair when the others sat down. He swallowed hard before he said, "Mr. Dan, I have decided." He swallowed again. "I will stay with Uncle Anthony and Aunt Beth and go to Cokesbury College to learn to be a travelin' preacher like you."